Please return/renew this item by the
last date shown to avoid a charge.
Books may also be renewed by phone
and Internet. May not be renewed if
required by another reader.

www.libraries.barnet.gov.uk

BARNET
LONDON BOROUGH

ILLUSTRATED BY PAUL DAVIDSON

Franklin Watts
First published in Great Britain in 2018
by The Watts Publishing Group

ISBN 978 1 4451 5936 2
ebook ISBN 978 1 4451 5937 9
Library ebook ISBN 978 1 4451 5938 6

1 3 5 7 9 10 8 6 4 2

Printed in Great Britain

MIX
Paper from
responsible sources
FSC® C104740
www.fsc.org

Franklin Watts
An imprint of
Hachette Children's Group
Part of The Watts Publishing Group
Carmelite House
50 Victoria Embankment
London EC4Y 0DZ

An Hachette UK Company
www.hachette.co.uk

www.franklinwatts.co.uk

Mission Statement

You are the hero of this mission.

Each section of this book is numbered. At the end of most sections, you will have to make a choice. The choice you make will take you to a different section of the book.

Some of your choices will help you to complete your mission successfully. But if you make the wrong choice, death may be the best you can hope for! Because even that is better than being UNDEAD and becoming a slave of the monsters you have sworn to destroy!

Dare you go up against a world of monsters?

All right, then.

Let's see what you've got...

Introduction

You are an agent of **G.H.O.S.T.** — Global Headquarters Opposing Supernatural Threats.

Our world is under constant attack from supernatural horrors that lurk in the shadows. It's your job to make sure they stay there.

You have studied all kinds of monsters, and know their habits and behaviour. You are an expert in disguise, able to move among monsters in human form as a spy. You are expert in all forms of martial arts. G.H.O.S.T. has supplied you with weapons, equipment and other assets that make you capable of destroying any supernatural creature.

G.H.O.S.T.

You are based at Arcane Hall, a spooky mansion. Your butler, Cranberry, is another G.H.O.S.T. agent who assists you in your adventures, providing you with information and backup.

Your life at Arcane Hall is comfortable and peaceful; but you know that at any moment, the G.H.O.S.T. High Command can order you into action in any part of the world...

Go to 1.

1

You are in the Phantom Flyer, returning to Arcane Hall, when Cranberry calls.

"We have a situation, agent. A tour party to the Holberg caves in Switzerland has gone missing. HQ suspects a vampire infestation. Divert to Zurich airport," he says.

You change course and run an Internet search on the Holberg Caves:

VISIT THE
HOLBERG CAVES
SWITZERLAND'S PREMIER
TOURIST ATTRACTION
MILES OF TUNNELS
MAJESTIC CAVERNS
ENCHANTED GROTTOES
BOOK TICKETS NOW!

You know that back at Arcane Hall, Cranberry is searching all G.H.O.S.T.'s data for information.

"Remind me what we have on vampires," you say. "They're tough opponents, right?"

"You bet!" says Cranberry cheerfully. "Very fast and agile: but they can be destroyed by fire, holy water or a stake through the heart. Garlic slows them down. UV rays from your flashlight or grenades work too, as does sunlight — though usually, like garlic, that just weakens them. Only the light of dawn kills them instantly."

You check your flightplan. "I'm starting my final approach to Zurich."

"I'll have a fully-equipped Spook Truck waiting for you. Good luck!"

From the airport, you drive into the mountains. At the entrance to the caves, you are stopped by a police cordon. You show your G.H.O.S.T. ID and are allowed through. You collect your 3V and other equipment from the Spook Truck.

You enter the caves and make your way cautiously through dimly-lit tunnels and caverns. You check your comms link.

"Cranberry," you call softly, "can you hear me?" There is no reply. You are too deep underground for the comms link to work. You're on your own.

Suddenly, you stop dead. Ahead of you is a pathetic huddle of bodies — the missing tourists. You glimpse movement in the shadows. There's something out there!

To use your 3V, go to 12.

To shoot holy water at the intruder, go to 25.

To fire a rocket-propelled stake at the intruder, go to 37.

2

"I'll head for Lucerne," you tell Cranberry.

"Are you mad?" he demands. "Mount Pilatus is a mountain resort — the clue is in the name! The vampires who are heading there must be the ones who fed first — the strongest! They're almost ready to fly. The others will need to find more victims before they are ready to follow, but if you let these get away, they'll spread the plague of vampirism all over the world!"

You speak sharply to hide your embarrassment. "All right! I'll go after them first."

Go to 14.

3

You aim the RPS launcher, but with clubbers panicking and running for cover, you daren't fire for fear of hitting innocent people. What's more, the vampires are VERY quick. Two grab you and smash your RPS, holding you helpless while a third leaps to the attack.

Go to 29.

4

"There's only one chance," you tell Cranberry. "If
I fly to Milan from Zurich, I can get there first."

The fog is getting denser and the drive to
Zurich airport seems to take forever. You arrive
to find that the Phantom Flyer is ready for you
but the fog has closed the airport. Air Traffic
Control will not allow you to take off, and you
know that the vampires have got away!

You've mist your last chance! Go back to 1.

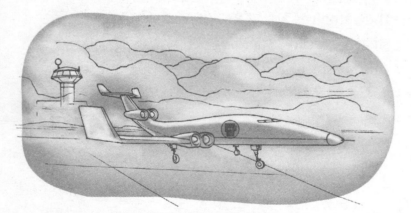

5

You draw your HWG and open fire.

But the vampire is already soaking wet — the
moment the pellets burst, the holy water is

diluted by the water of the cave. The vampire isn't even slowed down. It grasps your shoulders in an unbreakable grip, opens its mouth wide and lunges for your throat.

Go to 29.

6

You attack the nearest vampire. After a short struggle, you succeed in plunging a stake into its heart, and it crumbles into dust.

But during the fight, the Brood Leader has managed to get behind you. Now he pins your arms to your sides in an unbreakable grip. You are helpless!

Go to 29.

7

You fire your semi-automatic HWG at the couple. Pellets burst, soaking them and staining the wallpaper.

But the holy water has no effect (except to make them breathless and angry). These people look harmless — they can't be vampires.

The old couple curse and wave their arms about in protest. With a sinking feeling, you check the room number.

Go to 38.

8

You fire at the vampires, who burst into flame. So does the bridge!

"You maniac!" howls Cranberry. "Using a flame gun on a wooden bridge? What were you thinking?"

You wonder that yourself as you leap from the bridge to avoid being roasted alive, into the churning waters of the river. Your equipment drags you down. The freezing water closes over your head.

Don't be so wet! Go back to 1.

9

Your RPS takes out one vampire, but you can't turn the clumsy weapon to aim at the second target before the other one is upon you. With unhuman strength it clasps your shoulders and forces your head back — you are helpless!

Go to 29.

10

At this time of night, the Glacier Garden is closed. You climb over the surrounding fence and switch on your 3V. All seems quiet. You check your equipment and realise you are running out of rocket propelled stakes.

You follow a wooden walkway until you come to a deep, smooth-sided hole covered by an awning. You lean on the rail and look down into it. You can see nothing in the shadows. You turn away — and at that moment, a vampire hiding in the hole springs out, knocking you off your feet.

To use your HWG, go to 39.
To use your RPS, go to 24.

11

You arrive in the lobby just behind the fleeing vampires. One races for the front entrance, and you bring it down with an RPS. The other two dive into the restaurant. Ignoring screaming diners and shocked waiters, you chase after them and fire. One vampire collapses onto the sweet trolley and disintegrates. The other knocks over a fondue set and catches fire. The room is filled with panic and the smell of burning cheese.

Ignoring the chaos, you rush outside and look up — just in time to see the remaining two vampires launch themselves from the roof and disappear into the darkness.

Bad decision, Hunter. Go back to 1.

12

Your 3V reveals that the lurking figure is not a vampire.

"Who are you?" you call.

The figure approaches with hands raised. "I'm a police doctor. I heard you coming and hid — I thought whoever attacked these people might come back."

You show her your ID. "Let's see what's happened here."
Go to 43.

13

You check the map, and take a road that runs alongside the railway line.

You drive with one hand, fitting the last three rounds of RPS into the launcher. The road is dangerous in the fog, but as you head into the mountains it starts to clear. To your relief, you see the lights of the train in a cutting below you.

A moment later, to your horror, you realise that the road ahead is coming to a sharp bend that will take it away from the tracks.

To jump out of the Spook Truck and try to land on the train roof, go to 36.

To continue to follow the train, go to 22.

14

You head for Mount Pilatus and arrive at the valley station of the cog railway that runs up the steep side of the mountain.

As you ride in the slow, clicking carriage, Cranberry gives you an update.

"The vampires you're tracking have disappeared off the VROOM screen — it only works when they're out in the open, so they must

be in a building — a hotel or restaurant maybe."

You reload your RPS launcher.

"Don't sweat it. I'll find them."

"Make it quick," says Cranberry. "Remember, they have already fed on the tourists' blood in the caves and could be ready to fly at any minute. You must stop them!"

Leaving the train, you head for the nearest hotel. You enter the lobby. To one side is a busy restaurant; in front of you is a reception desk.

To enter the restaurant, go to 34.

To speak to the receptionist, go to 45.

15

You switch the HWG to "automatic fire" and spray the attacking vampires with high velocity holy water pellets. One collapses, writhing; but panicking clubbers get in the way of your shots, and the other two flee from the club.

You follow them along the waterfront to the famous Spreuerbrücke — the old covered bridge across the river Reuss. The wooden roof creates many shadows, but you can see that the triangular frames are painted with dancing skeletons. How appropriate, you think.

To cut off the vampires' escape, go to 23.

To follow them onto the bridge, go to 40.

16

Not wanting to waste ammo, you hesitate. Then you remember that vampires have no reflection in a mirror. It's too late! The vampire leaps on you, forcing you back against a pillar.

Go to 29.

17

You fire your RPS. As the stake penetrates its heart, the vampire explodes into a cloud of dust.

But even as you breathe a sigh of relief, two more vampires erupt from the lake and hurl themselves towards you. They are already soaked, so holy water won't have any effect. You have two rounds left in the RPS. You also have your EGS garlic-firing gun, and your flame pistol.

To use your RPS again, go to 9.

To use the EGS, go to 47.

To use the flame pistol, go to 33.

18

You send RPS rounds into three of the vampires,
destroying them. But now you are out of
ammunition.

Before you can switch to another weapon, the
remaining vampires are upon you! Two hold you
captive, while the third attacks!

Go to 29.

19

The souvenir shop is full of plastic cuckoo clocks,
printed T-shirts and Swiss chalet snow globes.
You ask the shopkeeper whether he has seen
anything suspicious.

"Yes," he says, "someone ran in and went into
the stockroom. I'll show you."

He leads you to a door at the back of the shop.
You go through, HWG at the ready. You hear a
click as the door shuts behind you. You try the
handle — it is locked. You are trapped!

All your weapons are designed to take out
vampires, not open doors! Despite the risk of
setting off a rocket charge in a small room, you
are about to try an RPS round when the door

bursts open and four vampires pile in. The RPS takes out one but the others grab you. The shopkeeper follows them in, smiling to reveal his fangs. He is a vampire in disguise!

"Hello, Hunter," he says. "Here's a souvenir you won't forget!" He lunges for your neck.

Go to 29.

20

You pull the emergency lever and the train judders to a stop, still in the tunnel.

The Brood Leader gives a harsh laugh. "What was that supposed to achieve?"

You make no answer. A vampire emerges from hiding. It, and the other vampire hold you captive while the Brood Leader approaches you, fangs gleaming.

There is a sound of running footsteps and a guard appears. "Is there a problem, sir?" he asks.

"Yes," says the Brood Leader smoothly, pointing at you. "This man broke a window. My associates have restrained him. You may tell the driver he can continue."

No human can resist the power of a vampire. The guard gives a hurried nod, and scuttles away. "I allowed the weaker members of our nest to feed first," says the Brood Leader. "I am glad I waited — it will make your blood taste all the sweeter." He eyes you hungrily and licks his lips as the train starts to move again. "See, Hunter?" mocks the Brood Leader. "The delay you caused was not significant."

You grin at him. "You think?"

The train bursts out of the tunnel, straight into the first rays of the rising sun. You have delayed it just long enough. The vampires turn to face their doom. They scream — and erupt into clouds of shimmering dust that are sucked out from the open window and scattered to the winds.

Go to 50.

As soon as you have finished checking the cave, you give the Swiss police the all-clear and call Cranberry. Quickly, you explain the situation.

"I'm checking the VROOM," he says.

You slide into the driver's seat and activate the screen for the Vampire Radar (Outdoor Operation Mode). This detects vampires by comparing heat signatures with movement. If a target is moving but has no body heat it's a vampire. The screen shows a satellite image, on which red dots are moving. You count the dots — there are twenty-four.

"Most of them are heading for the city of Lucerne," says Cranberry. "But five have broken away in the direction of Mount Pilatus."

To head for Lucerne, go to 2.

To head for Mount Pilatus, go to 14.

22

You haul on the wheel and the truck skids around the bend. You glance down at the train just as it enters a tunnel.

You check the map — to get back to the tracks, you face miles of detour. You will never catch the train now. The vampires have escaped!

You've run out of road! Go back to 1.

23

You call Cranberry. "Send the Spook Truck to the other end of the bridge."

"Roger."

You wait until the truck arrives. There is a blast of light as Cranberry switches on its headlights and searchlights, all especially equipped with UV bulbs. No vampire is getting past that!

You make your way across the bridge. Thanks to the Spook Truck's lights, you glimpse movement as the vampires drop from the roof, one each side of you.

To us the flame gun on them, go to 8.

To use the UV flashlight, go to 49.

You fire and the vampire explodes into dust. You check behind you as another vampire races to the attack. An instant later you are in a hand-to-hand struggle as the creature tries to force you over the rail and into the hole. Knowing that the fall will kill you, you find reserves of strength and fight back, taking a hand-stake from your pouch. You thrust the point into the vampire's heart, destroying it.

You glimpse shadowy movement in an arched doorway — the entrance to a mirror maze. You slip through it. Using your flashlight to locate a switch-box, you turn on the lights. Immediately, you are surrounded by multiple images of yourself. Some are distorted, making you look incredibly short or impossibly tall. Lights between the mirrors flash and change colour, adding to your confusion.

A vampire appears in front of you — but is it really there, or is it just a reflection?

To fire an RPS at the vampire, go to 41.

To hold your fire, go to 16.

25

You raise the HWG and fire holy water pellets at the hidden figure.

"Ow!" cries a voice from the darkness. "That stings!"

"Sorry," you call, "I thought you were a vampire!"

"Thanks!" The woman comes forward and checks your ID. "I'm a police doctor."

You indicate the bodies. "Let's see what happened here."

Go to 43.

26

You put down the RPS launcher, raise your EGS gun and fire. The garlic pellets spread out, knocking both vampires off their feet. As they writhe and scream, you finish them off with hand-stakes from your equipment pouch.

"Three to go," says Cranberry. "How many assets do you still have?"

You look for the RPS launcher, but it has disappeared! A lurch of the train must have made it fall off the roof. You check your remaining equipment with a sinking heart. You lost your holy water gun and UV grenades when you jumped for the train. You have just two hand-stakes left — and your UV flashlight.

"Oh, dear," says Cranberry. "Still, never say die!"

You check your 3V and swing down into the carriage. Two vampires are waiting for you. By his clothing and air of authority, you recognise the taller as the Brood Leader — the most dangerous of all.

He laughs. "Vampire Hunters used to be more formidable opponents. This is the end of the line for you."

You check your watch. It is only a few minutes until dawn.

The sound of the train gets louder as it enters a tunnel.

To attack the vampires hand-to-hand, go to 6.

To pull the emergency lever to stop the train, go to 20.

To use the UV flashlight, go to 32.

You follow the vampires up the stairs. By the time you burst out onto the roof, they are flapping clumsily away. You bring them both down with shots from your RPS.

Knowing that there is no time to waste, you race back to the lobby and ask where the others went.

The receptionist points. "They were heading for the cable car."

You follow the escaping vampires to the station. You see them getting into a cable car; but by the time you get there, their gondola has already left, and they are too far away for a good shot.

To take the next car, go to 31.

To slide down the cable, go to 46.

Cranberry's voice snaps over your comms link. "Get moving, Agent!"

"Give me a minute," you protest. "I can't see."

"You haven't got a minute! There are five

vampires left — and they're heading for the main railway station. They mustn't get away!"

Groaning and shaking your head to try and clear your vision, you stagger out of the maze and make your way back to the Spook Truck.

"I'm checking the Swiss Railways computers. They've just issued five tickets for the overnight train to Milan. If the vampires get to a city that size, we'll never find them!"

Even driving like a maniac, you arrive on the station platform just in time to see the Milan train disappearing into the fog that has started to descend.

To fly to Milan, go to 4.

To follow the train in the Spook Truck, go to 13.

29

The vampire plunges its fangs into your neck. You cannot break free! You feel the poison of its bite coursing through your veins.

You can only hope you will not survive — because if you do, you too will be a vampire, one of the undead monsters you have sworn to destroy!

Go back to 1.

30

You switch your HWG to "automatic" and open fire. But the mirrors are in the way and their confusing reflections spoil your aim. The vampires are splashed with holy water from bursting pellets, but none takes a direct hit that would destroy it.

The vampires pull back. You realise they are leading you deeper into the maze, away from the exit. You must make sure that none escape!

To switch to the RPS, go to 18.

To use a UV grenade, go to 48.

31

You leap into the next car but you can only watch helplessly as the vampires ahead prise open the door of their gondola and fly away into the night.

You got the vampires into a flap, but it wasn't enough! Go back to 1.

32

You shine your UV flashlight on the vampires.
They hiss with fury and cringe back.

But you have forgotten that five vampires
caught the train. The last one has been hiding —
and now it leaps out of the shadows, knocking
the flashlight from your hand and wrapping its
arms around you in an unbreakable grip.

Go to 29.

33

You send a sheet of flame roaring towards the vampires. They scream, but keep on coming. The water in their clothing is protecting them from the flame!

Before you can switch weapons, the first vampire reaches you and clasps you in a grip of iron. The second lunges for your throat.

Go to 29.

34

You stride into the restaurant wearing your
visor and armed to the teeth. The vampires,
hidden among the diners, spot you at once and
transform. The restaurant immediately descends
into chaos. Managers, waiters and hotel guests
flee for their lives.

You cannot use your weapons; there are too

many people in the way. It takes a long time to calm the situation — too long.

You see five shapes fly past the windows of the restaurant. By the time you have elbowed your way clear of the panicking crowd, the vampires have disappeared into the darkness, and there is no way you can follow.

The birds — er, vampires — have flown!
Go back to 1.

35

You call Cranberry. "Can you set the Spook Truck for self-drive mode and send it to meet me at the end of the cable car?"

"Copy that. The other vampires have reached Lucerne."

You pick up the Spook Truck and head for the city.

"The vampires have disappeared off the VROOM," says Cranberry. "I tracked them to the waterfront: then they must have taken cover."

You park at the point where the vampires disappeared. The nearest doors lead to a souvenir shop and a nightclub.

To check out the souvenir shop, go to 19.

To go into the nightclub, go to 44.

36

"Take over!" you tell Cranberry. You open the door, and leap for the roof.

You land heavily. Some of your equipment breaks free and is lost. You nearly roll across the roof and over the other side, but you manage to stop yourself. You look up to see the Spook Truck sail right over the train, smash into the valley below and erupt into a fireball.

"Great driving!" you mutter.

"Sorry," says Cranberry. "Duck!"

"What? Why?"

"Because you're going into a tunnel."

You drop face-down on the roof just in time. When the train comes out of the tunnel, you hear a carriage window being smashed just below you. Two vampires climb onto the roof.

To use the RPS on the vampires, go to 42.

To fight them hand-to-hand, go to 26.

37

You fire a round from our RPS launcher. Your aim is good. The target collapses with a cry.

But when you reach the fallen figure, you see a lot of blood. A vampire should have collapsed into dust.

You give a horrified groan. You have seriously injured a human being. You check her ID — she's a doctor, working with the Swiss police.

You are in deep trouble. The Director General will have your badge for this!

You race back to the cave entrance for help. Police and paramedics run into the caverns. Seconds later, you are in handcuffs.

Think before you shoot! Go back to 1.

38

You turn the list of room numbers over and groan aloud. You were reading it upside down! You should have gone to room 9!

You open your mouth to apologise — but at that moment, you hear thundering feet in the corridor behind you. The vampires are escaping!

You tumble out of the room and follow the

fleeing vampires until they reach a staircase. Two go up, heading for the roof. The others head down, towards the lobby.

To follow the vampires heading for the roof, go to 27.

To follow those heading for the lobby, go to 11.

39

You raise your HWG and fire. The vampire falls writhing to the floor. But as you reach for a stake to finish it off, another vampire jumps you from behind. You cannot reach your weapons. You are helpless.

Go to 29.

40

It is very dark on the bridge. Even your 3V is little help.

You have not gone far when two vampires drop from the roof beams, knocking your HWG over the parapet and into the swollen river. One grabs you from behind, the other lunges for your throat.

Go to 29.

You fire, and the vampire disintegrates: but now you only have three RPS rounds left.

You look up to see more vampires dodging between the mirrors, hoping to catch you unawares. You think there are five, but you cannot be sure.

To continue to use your RPS, go to 18.
To switch to your HWG, go to 30.

42

You scramble to your knees, raise the RPS launcher and fire. But the swaying of the train spoils your aim. All three shots miss their targets — and now you are out of ammo.

Go to 26.

43

"These people have been drained of blood. And look at this." You show the doctor that each victim has two puncture holes in the neck. "The mark of a vampire."

She shakes her head. "Vampires are a myth."

"There are still nests of vampires all over the world," you tell her, "lying dormant. Something must have disturbed them here — maybe cave explorers. Now they're out of the coffin, and hungry for blood!"

"But doesn't their bite turn people into vampires?"

"If they drain their victim, they kill them. If they take less blood, they turn the victim into another vampire. Members of a newly-awakened nest would want to create new vampires — but if they were starving..."

The doctor stands. "I must go and report this."

"I'll check the caves. I'm guessing the vampires have left already — maybe."

You set off deeper into the caves. The lights are dimmer here. You arrive at a flooded cave, and wade through knee-deep water — until a vampire breaks the surface right at your feet and leaps to the attack!

To use your Holy Water Gun, go to 5.

To fire a Rocket Propelled Stake, go to 17.

You put on your 3V and enter the nightclub.

The club is crowded but your visor instantly reveals that there are four vampires among the crowd. You have a clear shot at one and take him out with an RPS. In the ensuing panic, the others come at you.

To use the RPS again, go to 3.

To use the HWG, go to 15.

You show the receptionist your ID and ask whether anyone has checked in recently.

"Yes," he says. "Five people, wearing old-fashioned clothes. They paid for their rooms in gold coins."

"I bet they did," you say. "Can you write down their room numbers, please?"

You creep along the hotel corridor to the first room on the list — number 6. You take a deep breath, kick the door open, and burst in.

And old couple are sitting up in bed. They cry out in terror.

To fire your HWG at the couple, go to 7.

To check the room number, go to 38.

Leaping onto the top of the next car, you unsling your RPS launcher and use it to slide down the cable towards the vampires.

You land on top of the vampires' gondola. The panicking creatures prise open the door and try to fly away. You take out all 3 with your RPS. As the clouds of ex-vampire drift away, you drop into the gondola, gasping for breath.

Go to 35.

You point your EGS gun at the first vampire, and pull the trigger. The gun roars and the creature is peppered with garlic. As it staggers back, you fire again at the second.

The garlic isn't enough to kill the vampires, but it slows them down. You pull a couple of hand-stakes from your equipment pouch, and race to the attack, hand to hand. Seconds later, your attackers collapse into piles of dust.

You stay alert as you cross the flooded cavern, but there are no further attacks. Beyond the lake you find a cavern that looks as if its entrance has been recently disturbed. Inside, resting in wall niches, are a number of stone coffins.

You count them. There are twenty-seven. You have accounted for three vampires — so there are twenty-four still at large.

Go to 21.

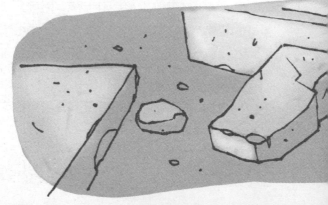

48

You roll a UV grenade towards the vampires. It explodes in a silent, blinding flash of light.

This weapon would not normally be powerful enough to destroy even a single vampire outright — but here in the maze, its rays bounce between the mirrors with the speed of light. The vampires scream as they are torn to atoms.

Go to 28.

49

You shine your UV flashlight into the eyes of each of the vampires in turn. Already weakened by the lights from the truck, they are blinded and stagger about helplessly. You snatch hand-stakes from your equipment pouch and finish them off.

"Well done, Agent," says Cranberry. "Eleven down, thirteen to go."

"Unlucky for some," you mutter.

"I've tracked eight to the Glacier Garden."

"Great!"

Go to 10.

50

The train rattles on. You slump into a seat.

"Well done, Agent," says Cranberry. "The Director General says you can take some downtime. She reckons twenty-four hours will be quite enough. So what will you do in Milan? Take in an opera at La Scala?" He sings, "*Vesti la giubba...*"

"Stop strangling cats," you say, "and book me a ticket for the football at the San Siro stadium. AC Milan are playing Barcelona."

"You have terrible taste," complains Cranberry, "for a hero."

EQUIPMENT

Phantom Flyer: For fast international and intercontinental travel, you use the Phantom Flyer, a supersonic business jet crammed full of detection and communication equipment and weaponry.

Spook Truck: For more local travel you use one of G.H.O.S.T.'s fleet of Spook Trucks — heavily armed and armoured SUVs you requisition from local agents.

3V — Vampire Vision Visor

RPS — Rocket Propelled Stake

HWGs — Holy Water Guns

UV FLASHLIGHT

UV GRENADES

EGS — Eat Garlic, Sucker!

FLAME PISTOL

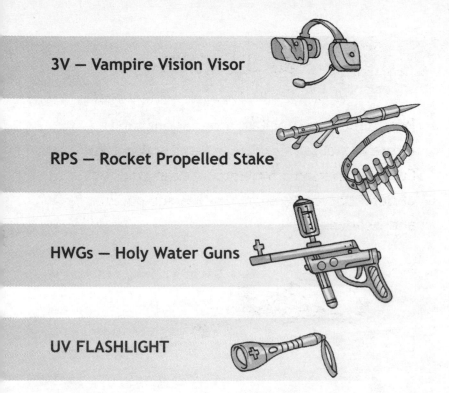

MONSTER HUNTER

GHOST

STEVE BARLOW ◇ STEVE SKIDMORE
Illustrated by PAUL DAVIDSON

EDGE

I HERO

You are taking a well-earned day off from saving the world. You are on a private tour of the Tower of London, home to the Crown jewels of the British monarchy.

Your guide is a Yeoman of the Guard. He is holding a pike and tells you of the Tower's gruesome history.

"Many people were executed at the Tower, including three queens!" he says. "And they were not happy about it!"

"How do you know?" you ask, jokingly. "Did they tell you?"

"As a matter of fact, yes they did." He stares at you strangely. "Do you believe in ghosts?"

You nod.

"I'm glad to hear it!" He emits a low growling noise and you realise that you can see through his body! It is a ghost but the pike he's holding is real and he's pointing it at you!

Continue the adventure in:

GHOST

About the 2Steves

"The 2Steves" are
Britain's most popular
writing double act
for young people,
specialising in comedy
and adventure. They
perform regularly in schools and libraries,
and at festivals, taking the power of words
and story to audiences of all ages.

Together they have written many books,
including the *I HERO Immortals* and *iHorror* series.

About the illustrator:
Paul Davidson

Paul Davidson is a British
illustrator and comic book artist.

I HERO Legends — collect them all!

ATHENA

978 1 4451 5234 9 pb
978 1 4451 5235 6 ebook

BEOWULF

978 1 4451 5225 7 pb
978 1 4451 5226 4 ebook

KING ARTHUR

978 1 4451 5231 8 pb
978 1 4451 5232 5 ebook

FREYA

978 1 4451 5237 0 pb
978 1 4451 5238 7 ebook

HERCULES

978 1 4451 5228 8 pb
978 1 4451 5229 5 ebook

ROBIN HOOD

978 1 4451 5183 0 pb
978 1 4451 5184 7 ebook

Have you read the I HERO Toons series?

INVASION OF THE BOTTY SNATCHERS

978 1 4451 5927 0 pb
978 1 4451 5928 7 ebook

ENTER THE PENGUIN

978 1 4451 5924 9 pb
978 1 4451 5925 6 ebook

KILLER CUSTARD

978 1 4451 5930 0 pb
978 1 4451 5931 7 ebook

KUNG FU KITTEN

978 1 4451 5918 8 pb
978 1 4451 5919 5 ebook

ROBIN HAMSTER

978 1 4451 5921 8 pb
978 1 4451 5922 5 ebook

ATTACK of the ZOMBIE BUNNIES

978 1 4451 5873 0 pb
978 1 4451 5874 7 ebook

Also by the 2Steves...

978 1 4451 5104 5 pb
978 1 4451 5119 9 eBook

You are a skilled, stealthy ninja. Your village has been attacked by a warlord called Raiden. Now YOU must go to his castle and stop him before he destroys more lives.

978 1 4451 5101 4 pb
978 1 4451 5117 5 eBook

You are the Warrior Princess. Someone wants to steal the magical ice diamonds from the Crystal Caverns. YOU must discover who it is and save your kingdom.

4451 5103 8 pb
4451 5121 2 eBook

You are a magical unicorn. s Yin Yang has stolen Carmine, unicorn. Yin Yang wants to he colourful Rainbow Land. U must stop her!

978 1 4451 5102 1 pb
978 1 4451 5124 3 eBook

You are a spy, codenamed Scorpio. Someone has taken control of secret satellite laser weapons. YOU must find out who is responsible and stop their dastardly plans.